ESIDE MYSELF

© 2022 by Ashley Marie Farmer
Apocalypse Party
All rights reserved.

No part of this book may be reproduced or transmitted in any form or by any means, electronic or mechanical, including photocopying, recording, or by any information storage and retrieval system, without permission in writing from the copyright owner.

This is a work of fiction. Names, characters, places, and incidents either are the product of the author's imagination or are used fictitiously, and any resemblance to any actual person, living or dead, events, or locales is entirely coincidental.

Cover Design by Matthew Revert
Interior Design by Mike Corrao

ISBN: 978-1-954899-07-0

Beside Myself

Ashley Marie Farmer

Interior

PART ONE

THE LIGHT AT THE END OF THE TUNNEL
OF LOVE THE RIDGE
PROTEST
THE BAT
BEHIND THE BARN OVERLOOKING
MOTHER'S REQUIEM FOR RAIN
SON NAMELESS
COFFIN WATER
SNOW/SUNRISE/AMBULANCE
DMV
HAPPY HOUR
BESIDE MYSELF
THEN I AWOKE TO WHAT I KNOW
TORNADO WARNING

PART TWO

LIMELIGHT
CONSIDER THE BLIND FISH
DRIVE-IN
YOU WATCHED THE PARTY FROM THE CHANDELIER
NEIGHBOR LOSES HIS KEYS IN THE DARK
BROTHER(S)
RADIO LAKE
SUMMER ACCIDENT
WHERE EVERYONE IS A STAR

PART THREE

PILLAR OF SALT
TEMPORARY RIVER
MAN FOUND DEAD IN GRAVEYARD
NEIGHBOR RECALLS THE ACTORS
THE TIGER
THE WOMEN
STAR CHILDREN
UNTITLED WITH FATHER
GAME SHOW
NEIGHBOR CONSIDERS THE YARD AT MIDNIGHT
UFO
PINK WATER
ASSEMBLED
PUTTING THE NEIGHBORS TO BED
RENDEZVOUS
PERFECT CHRISTMAS
DIARY OF AN EX-PRECEDENT

PART FOUR

THE HOLE
ELEGY FOR SATISFACTION
STILL LIFE WITH NEIGHBOR
AT THE BEACH
SO MANY BONES
IN THE SHAPE OF A-OK
SLEEP
BULLSHIT FENCES
IMAGINARY WHEAT
FORTY-LOVE
THE NEW YEAR
HORSESHOES

"God! This town is like a fairy tale. Everywhere you turn there's mystery and wonder. And I'm just a child playing cops and robbers forever. Please forgive me if I cry."

— James Tate, "It Happens Like This"

PART ONE

THE LIGHT AT THE END OF THE TUNNEL OF LOVE

I'D ASKED JAIL ABOUT THE LIGHT at the end of the Tunnel of Love. "It isn't shaped like a heart," he said. We slugged cheap chardonnay on my fractured front porch. We imagined a high school football game taking place on the lawn. Every now and then Jail cheered for the cheerleaders.

We got into the spirit. My yard is close to the fairgrounds, so it wasn't a stretch to pretend the screams from rollercoasters were fans cheering. Jail yelled as zero happened at the zero-yard line and a yellow Datsun slashed the road beyond the driveway. Exhaust traveled into the cornfields. The grass filled with fireflies, nubs of bugs blinking.

Jail had gone to jail for tampering with courthouse lamps. That's why we called him Jail. He said, "The light at the end of the Tunnel of Love is like lightning hitting your legs, but healthier. You leave lifted." A firefly lit on his thumb. "I'd love to crush this," he said, but didn't.

"Let's go for a ride," he said. "We'll never win with this much time left." He scooped his keys and stood.

But then we did it, we resurrected. Twenty-nine seconds left. An interception. Number thirty-four ran it back, beyond zero, beyond the bullshit fence, back through yesterday, the last six months, so far back that Jail and I hadn't met, so far back that I'd never even happened.

I stood. Jail screamed, "Get 'em, yes." I screamed, too, and the bodies falling through the amusement park screamed, and the naive, glimmering high school students screamed, and the fireflies blinked ignorant and sweet because no one who understood our town and this light wanted to harm them. It had been the summer of the lawn light power flickering in and out. It had been the summer of Tunnel of Love forgiveness. Fall wasn't almost over, and light, we had light.

THE RIDGE

ONE SISTER POLISHES the crystal hotel. She warms expensive air for guests or manifests cold when they request it. Our other sister fishes silver trout from the river. In the future, there might be more efficient ways for future guests or future rivers, but we don't discuss this. At night, from different yards in the valley, we wait for the moon to slide up behind The Ridge. A single dinner plate with names scratched in it.

I have one watery sister and another who's steady. One slugs cups of wine with nine o'clock pills. The other doesn't stutter in moonlight. I used to think things would get better. I used to think I'd be the best sister. We used to get together and say, "Hey, we're fine, aren't we, we are," but not anymore.

My mother used to drive us up to The Ridge, a neighborhood that overlooked ours. My favorite house was a lavender cube with pink windows. My grown self flickered like heat in the kitchen. I imagine the owner imagined what I imagined: that she lived in the successful future.

If you lived on The Ridge, you had two backyards: your lawn, and the valley below your lawn. The valley was filled with cheap yards like ours where we did dirt work on weekends with rakes and shovels. Along the bottom of The Ridge was a river, which kept people from scrabbling upward or tumbling down too far like boulders.

When we were kids in the valley, we used to wake up in the moonlit morning. Our mother cued music to end our sleep—a song about looking up and forward and dreaming. Before our eyes even opened, we floated from bed and out the sliding glass door. Willing ourselves to rise up toward we didn't know what, or what for.

PROTEST

WE RIOT AT THE BOTTOM of the mountain. We raise our signs. Our voices hurtle upward and hit the window, ineffective as rat-shot or messenger pigeons because there are only two of us. The others never show up.

When the powerful man comes out, liquid-faced, cheeks a mean sunset, he yells, "Why are you doing this?" We throw our signs and the ivy on his house withers black. The sky crumples, darkens. It will again register its complaint.

He raises one fist, then the other, then loses his balance. He rolls through the brush and lands in a cloud at our feet. We bend, unzip the heavy costume down the side of his body.

Beneath the padding: a smaller man, curled like a question mark.

THE BAT

THE PROBLEM WITH THE BAT, you claimed, was it wasn't dead. The greater problem, I thought, was it wasn't quite alive. We carried it in a box to the park, behind the dark gazebo, knowing the dark gazebo near the shore is where things give up, where things get claimed, where the anonymous do the claiming. We had both done that, on either end like a seesaw, and now we were at an impasse. Hadn't we met here? I couldn't stand to go back, not with this quivering black body in a shoebox, not with that wide black yawn approaching in the sky. Would it be better if it were small? you asked. Like a bug? you asked. Would it be better if we had poison? If we could make it breathe? If we could stomp it out like a fire? I didn't answer. As we approached the wooden steps, my mind drifted to the efficient angles of boats sleeping in the harbor, their delicate math solving and unsolving. We left the bat on a bench. It might have rained after, though I never saw you again. But the boats, do you remember?

BEHIND THE BARN, OVERLOOKING

I HEAR THE BLACK CLOCK HISS: it's nine again. Outside the house, it could be anybody's guess. It is too dark to hear time out there, and there are too many trees capped with snow to know the difference. The moon is anybody's guess and anybody could be waiting for me. A conversation, at best. A walk under anybody's guess.

Behind the barn, overlooking the dark pond, the idea of a neighbor rocks in a chair. He is waiting for me. In his lap: a left-handed deck of dark cards. In his pocket, an envelope filled with bills. There is always so much surprise along the path to the barn. My idea of a neighbor is patient, rocking. His best guess is that I will press tonight toward the edge of dark water.

REQUIEM FOR RAIN

BIRDS SPARK TO FLIGHT in twelve directions. They smolder, tinged with injury: the woods behind the house are still on fire. I press the polished window and heat ascends the lifeline of my palm. Branches torch and crack through months of evening dishes. But the fire fails to grow. It fails to diminish. It stays the same. For years I'll sing: *A fire is a fire is a fire*. The only song with lyrics I remember.

SON NAMELESS

I ONCE HAD A SON, a ghost who threw knives and suggested Coltrane as I slept. He was my son and he could bring hollow limbs to life with breath that slipped between my venetian blinds. His eyes were dark ponds for skipping stones or drowning. He was my son but blameless, no relation. He was a moth, thin as paper, an angel of two dimensions. And that lean, truth-telling cord I held like a kite string.

COFFIN WATER

WHEN I WAS A KID, my father warned me not to touch the coffin water. Coffin Water was a creek in the woods but it was also a condition. "You're not that kind of girl," he said. "Don't touch it and don't go wandering." Nobody wanted coffin water just like nobody wanted chicken pox or day blindness. If word got out that you'd swam in the creek, the counselor might call you in and the kids would slander behind their slates. I thought coffin water was a purple rash, something that could make Jesus hover over my bed where I'd sleep for a month until I woke up spilling gibberish and liking what I used to hate.

In the woods behind our house, I'd travel Coffin Water until I was dizzy. I'd speak to the water which was clear and tinkling and the opposite of purple. "Show me where to go," I'd ask and it would transmit advice. But I'm not going to share it here—I hope you understand why.

It always looked so clear to me, and sometimes I'd drink it. Coffin Water didn't taste like coffin water.

I'd been to one funeral ever.

I pictured the casket leaking, a slow drip at first, then a flood expelling mourners and their heart-shaped flowers through the church doors. I never saw coffins floating in Coffin Water. I never heard a single splinter.

Sometimes it dried up as I walked alongside it, cracking. Other times it switched routes and I'd exit the woods confused and too near the bar in the wet county one county over. I'd glimpse men smoking up dusk against a dangerous car. Inside the woods, the creek creaked "Get back here, girl, if you know what's good."

One day, father came home early from work. I was sitting on the back porch, breathless, my shirt so wet it was clear. It was clear where I'd been—even my mouth was damp, my hair. His face turned purple. "I never knew you were that kind of girl."

I wiped my lips and believed him.

I found out later that I didn't know much back then. Even later, I found out that my father didn't either. It turns out none of our fathers did, and still nobody has told them. How wrong they were, how mistaken, those fathers bruised and troubled by their thirsty girls.

SNOW/SUNRISE/AMBULANCE

WE'RE LUCKY when it comes to snow. In other words, the snow is warm. We can sit out front in lawn chairs as the sun rises and the snow piles soft and warm on our feet. The long white slope of yard is a naked body and we can't look away. Is this where we were sitting when the ambulance came? Wasn't the sunrise beautiful this morning? Wasn't this morning last night?

DMV

ON THE LAST DAY OF MY LIFE, before the incident that did not occur above some large body of water, I was summoned to take a driving test. This was in Kentucky, back when it was populated with ex-wives, the ghosts of ex-wives, widows, and other women whose hands didn't fit anywhere, mine included.

That morning, in the bathroom mirror, I noticed I'd gotten tame around the eyes. More troubling: someone had draped my living room furniture with sheets, preemptive.

The first part of the test was open-ended: "Anything I have to show for myself could fit in the trunk of my car," I wrote, and: "Anything but drowning." There were other lines along the same lines and there were some answers I couldn't be sure of—which hand signal, which window.

I spent the lunch break looking at my reflection in the shatterproof glass of the cashier's station. Pressed into a dress I had little to do with, I suddenly wanted to go swimming with my mother. I wanted to fold my dress into a box and push it down a river and race my long-gone mother to the opposite shore.

A man with a clipboard guided me outside for the driving portion. The sun had melted religious figures onto my dashboard, and though they weren't mine, I knew I would never be able to shake them. "You'll have to excuse me," said the man with a clipboard. "We had to use your car—there were a lot of people to test today." The crosses and virgins looked magical, heavy-handed. To show I had no hard feelings, I reached out to shake the gentleman's hand, but missed.

I took my place behind the wheel; he took his in the passenger's seat. "When traffic is clear," he said, "do whatever you think is best." Jesus had spread his liquid arms across the dash in a puddle of white, and I felt a hand on my neck. I remembered it from the mirror that morning, or from some time when men had not given up on us, but it was not a man's hand, and it was not my own, just a memory from some long-past day.

    Then there were hands everywhere: one guiding the car like a toy, one waving us toward the bridge, another pointing to the bank of the river. One to break our fall. One to take the distance out of anything it touched.

HAPPY HOUR

IN THE CITY I find more city. Deer vault from parking structure to parking structure. When I jangle my keys the animals tremble near concrete beams. It's so wild when the building shakes. I avoid mirrors, filing cabinets, windows. I use my arms to protect myself. In an emergency, the carpet beneath my desk becomes desert. I sift it for miles and I sweat through my jacket like an animal. My shoes are crammed with sand.

One day a train parked in the lobby, an accidental renovation of smoke and glass and crushed black granite. My neighbor stepped from the train. He stepped through shards of his reflection then through mine, his face alive and tan, as though he'd been away on vacation. Happy hour began happening at the nearest outdoor assembly points, but who was smiling? Then the girders and skylights assembled again. They began their slow repair, just like us. Then neared repair. Nearer and nearer. Repairing.

BESIDE MYSELF

HOW I HAD COME TO THIS was nobody's business but my own: subscribing to the hollowed-out minutes of an empty movie theater on days that made few demands and offered even fewer rewards. Back then, a coat was something to be wrangled into. My profile was slack, slumping. The projection of my body toward the bus stop: weightless. If people asked, you could say my inclinations had been shaken out of me.

Back then the world was full of men in booths, producing tickets, pressing them into my palms. The satisfaction didn't last long: as soon as I clenched my fist, the men appeared around the corner to tear in half what they'd just bestowed. My pockets were populated with stubs suggesting an entrance or exit. I collected these for proof that I had been.

We're never the only ones. She was in the third row, collared with the tail of an animal. The tan lines on her fingers and wrists suggested a sudden repositioning to fortune. I obscured myself two rows behind her.

The dark darkened further. I felt the nudge of fur against my hand.

It's not like I was beside myself.

THEN I AWOKE TO WHAT I KNOW

THOSE SCRABBLED RINGS inside the trunks of ash and elm denote our histories and mine. If rainwater manages to sop it out, will the acres be renamed for arsonists or firefighters? No matter. It's our life, bundled like a dried-out bud, inside this house that brittles. We ache like tinder. We flare, all this kindling shoved inside a box of rooms together. Grab the hose and shovel, the radio. Someone call the river where we were dipped and soaked in something holier than water.

We fell backward, hair rippling in the current.

We floated golden in the forest. Now we're leaden, older.

In the woods, I found a stopwatch once and kept

it framed upon the mantel. I found a tattered map, the outline of my hand carved on it. One time, alone, I fell asleep and dreamed in clover: absent clothes, green grew across my body, thrust up around my thighs and between my naked fingers. I flowered, grew stiller than a Polaroid opening to light and all the years that touch it after. I'd never heard of being lonely, yet it was only me.

Then I awoke to what I know: the edges of others, sparked with need. Like a tree divested of its best leaves. Like a feather at my foot, no bird in sight.

TORNADO WARNING

THE RADIOS ARE LOADED with warning. The sky gets sick, rolls up its green belly. We go behind the shed where the water jugs are stored. Children's shadows slough off the bottom of the county pool. Each is a black cape. Someone blows a whistle and they disperse. The prison sleeps in the distance and the bony cows belong to no one. The neighbor knots a boat to a tree. His flag is a losing flag and has holes. Down at the track, ribboned hats fly away. Behind the shed it could be January or June. We wait like threads to be pulled.

PART TWO

LIMELIGHT

ON THE OUTSKIRTS OF THE EVENING, I looked for someone I might speak to plainly. The clerk clanged the register closed and said, "How do you plan to pay for this?" Like my father speaking to my mother via afterlife's short-wave radio and hatcheting through clay and stone, dying still to make things even at each end. Even now, assembling sense is like carrying a pigeon in a box. Like treading water down a fall. There was never enough: only want. At St. Anthony Hospital, I came three minutes close to being born into a prize. Instead I dozed, tardy, my right eye flourished with a fighter's shiner. My parents, already broke, suddenly somehow poorer. Today my horoscope portends zilch, zero, just says something about loving "limelight." So I sleep naked, unbuffered against the moon, pretending myself into a pool that someone thirsty will arrive at and bend down to.

CONSIDER THE BLIND FISH

EVERYONE MARRIED in July. I didn't know the guests I danced against. Certain gestures of wildlife are called "endemic." Locales: spot-on exotic, waterlogged with sunset. On someone else's post-wedding-day trip, I trekked toward freshwater springs with bathing-suited guests. We scrabbled down a ladder underground. We stood there sogged. Can you imagine materializing like water, a volcanic surprise?

The guide flashlighted toward a slim fish, absent eyes. He said, "Look, his body is as harmless as a butter knife." I, too, might have been named for what I lacked: soft hull revealing the dull blade in me. In the dark, the strangers' profiles approximated people I recalled. Intimates, you could say, from a little while ago.

The blind fish loops the same stalagmite for miles, growing wild in unremembering. My childhood pets were sprung from carnivals. The foundation of our attachments to them? Sticky quarters, desperate lobs, lens-corrected vision. Then no more: my parents ceased chancing affection on lives that insisted on expiring so quickly.

Some people (I don't know them) keep blind fish in tanks—bathed in light, their bodies become transparent. I reemerged into sunlight and passengered the red-eye home, horizontal across an unsold seat. I read that the pilot fish chaperones sharks across the bottom of the sea. Unlike the blind fish, they don't make good pets and are erratic when caught.

Our guide had asked us how we thought the blind fish mates. When we didn't answer, he told us it happens by accident.

DRIVE-IN

IT RAINED AGAINST A drive-in matinee about danger. M. and I were Friday with no school and there was above us some great beauty driving beautifully across the screen. We hadn't rented the speaker so we couldn't hear her over her fake convertible car moves and all those flat black trees rippling on canvas behind her. Our hearts on fire. Everywhere we'd driven that year, people asked what kind of women we were becoming. It was dangerous to know, dangerous to not know, and M. dabbed lipstick. Were we even minor beauties? Hardly. The woman's convertible rocked and the woman laughed her teeth because danger was still a distance she hadn't crossed and her face was covered in rainwater. M. had lost the title of her car in the rain. I had lost a map, I had lost an afternoon. I had almost lost my danger. The bottom corner of the screen ripped, pulled down by an unseen hand, and the woman parked at the edge of black trees started running. I wanted M. to drive me home in the rain. We couldn't understand the beauty's words, we couldn't remember a time when women drove convertibles without losing their smiles, when they couldn't get too far away in their fake cars, the trees from home so close they could always touch them. M. slid the bottle across the seat. The seats were leather. M. settled and the sun sunk. What kind of women were we becoming? M.'s car was just another car in the rain, her mom's, not even hers, and water had found its way in. "M.," I said, "Drive me home." The wet leather smelled alive. I didn't want to know the ending.

YOU WATCHED THE PARTY FROM THE CHANDELIER (OR HOW THE HOTEL LOBBY LOOKS LIKE A WORLD AND THE FACES A CONSTELLATION OF WAYS YOU HAVEN'T FAILED BUT COULD)

FROM THIS DISTANCE they could be celebrating birth, death, the end of the black plague—the marble floor is bright flesh with blue veins so convincing you'd bend to kiss it if you weren't clutching the wrist of distance itself. The body itself: more space than matter, and the space between bodies a long-distance phone call. How you will go home tonight with ceiling plaster in your hair knowing that up close clouds have holes and how a hand doesn't know emptiness until someone fills it. In the space between breaths I will call you: *come down*. It's not that I've figured it out, how distance can feel like perspective, space between subject and object so safe it startles the livid heart, which pauses as often as it beats. Oh, I've done it again, inserted myself into a party I'm no part of. I'm sorry, but I just want to be the moment in which you happen, and the crystal teardrops between your knees, quivering—

NEIGHBOR LOSES HIS KEYS IN THE DARK

HE SPILLS THE SLIM BRASS RING with little on it. No glint of key, no hint that his neighbor is awake. Streetlights are extinct. The moon: flimsy, faint, a cardboard fake. As for light enough to see, the stars are useless.

He presses his ear to the ground. The neighbor hears the local dreams, feels the tough earth tremor as they travel. He hears pairs of bodies twist like tree roots. Limbs twine. Dreamers trespassing into one another's minds.

His own bed behind the bolted door is smooth and empty. He could smash a window, but for what? The neighbor rolls onto his back. Stars: pushpins holding black fabric together. They keep him from falling apart.

BROTHER(S)

THEY WERE BORN TWO BROTHERS, but their shadows fused together. They combined in the woods. Their shiftings inextricable: when one brother broke into flood, the other broke into feather.

They tamed lions in the forest with leathers and sticks. They returned from the woods with soot on their knees and cheeks.

One brother has amber for eyes, sap in which the hobbled past gets stuck. The other has cold gray river rock.

Even though they're the same, they're not always together: one brother cries alone in a diner booth while the other smokes cigarettes as he laps the track. At school, they've been assigned separate mirrors, separate handshakes. They gauge girls at opposite reflecting pools. One brother drags around a filthy guitar. The other pats his pockets for disappearing ink.

When the bell rings, they overlap beyond the chain-link fence.

At dusk, they flame paper planes out the window. Some months a bird sparks, other seasons it doesn't. Once, the lawn beyond the front porch flared and they were made to walk across the bridge as punishment.

They're out there still, toeing careful, careful while wind whips the river below them. You'd know the bridge, it's a famous one. It either binds two states together or estranges them.

RADIO LAKE

RADIO LAKE said *STAY AWAY*. The water sighed *WARNING*. It suggested we didn't know best. But on a cold moon we'd arrive at its edges and hear radios humming beneath wet branches.

We swam in Radio Lake despite the dangers. We thought we understood the static.

Sister and I would swig some sour fizz and strip beneath the stars. She'd dive first. I'd slip down instead to split the surface because I was nervous. The radio static buzzed us like good pollution.

One day at school, they divided the girls and guys into dim rooms. The desks that had always been desks felt miniature, and I touched a moon, a breast, a teardrop someone had carved with a pen. The screen flashed the shape of Radio Lake. There were parts blacked out, like sister stretched across her diving rock. The white screen told us to stay away from

Radio Lake. You should wait, they sighed. Care more about daylight songs, they begged.

We traveled the woods that night once our parents had vanished. We tramped branches and snagged sweaters. I floated my naked pulse in the still lake.

Then the white noise rose and sister shushed us.

At every edge of Radio Lake, headlights flipped up and we could see them inside, the men and women sketched against darkness like we'd suspected, except all of them were paired wrong, with others who belonged to others, and the music expressed misery, confusion. They sighed behind windows with damp eyes.

Sister covered her ears. I was almost grown then, almost gone.

SUMMER ACCIDENT

THEN THE JUNE ROAD VANISHED a girl I knew. Down our street, a black truck held the dent in its hood. Nights, I worried through a medical book. Studied the names of fractures: oblique, greenstick, buckle. I learned how to knot a tourniquet.

My girlfriends aspired to see the circus. To watch sequined women fling their bodies toward breathless men who'd catch them. From the driveway, I glimpsed a semi dragging a segment of funhouse off. I saw empty animal cages hauled away.

From the porch, I memorized the older neighbor boy on his skateboard ramp. His flushed face thrust above our fence then disappeared, only to reemerge a few feet over. For days, I counted him to one hundred and back down again.

The front yard oak tree rotted with sudden disease. We gutted its trunk in the dark and packed the wound with wet cement. A scourge of thin, yellow worms writhed in the branches. If you stood back, the leaves moved. If you stepped across the road, the whole thing looked alive.

ASHLEY MARIE FARMER

WHERE EVERYONE IS A STAR

I'D BEEN HIRED TO GUIDE children's bodies through air—kids shot through my palms mid-vault, my hands glancing torqued torsos, the horizontal fling of flexed ambitions. Above our tumbling routines and trampoline acts, the gym's red-lettered motto: WHERE EVERYONE IS A STAR. Manic kiddie soundtracks looped and shrilled as knots of party balloons burst, lingered in corners, manifested deadpan in the bathroom mirror. On breaks I knelt in the closet to pop palmfuls of nondrowsys from a blister pack. I'd return my smile to the mats, make mid-air grasps at those springy, unfinished forms. I was paid to catch girls against breaking.

I held several in my gaze at once, willing my attention to both expand and zero in. It was easy, my insides amphetamine-gleamy, razored out, point-sharpened, hollow, and that hollowness made space for instinct and reflex, not generalized feelings, not feelings about home, not the elaborate pain shocking my knee as I sprinted the mats. If a child's ankle tucked or if she hadn't chalked her hands enough, rare fractures eventualized. Cracks and the astonishing cries summoned whorls of red light to the parking lot. But mostly we were safe. I worked hard at that.

For ten hours a day I clowned the toddler crowds. They knew no longing, their soft bellies milk-filled and Lyrcra'd in expensive spangled leotards. Mothers spent good money. In the stands behind soundproof panels, each woman swelled: *Look at the child's burgeoning spatial awareness! The ease with which she forms relationships! Look at the accelerating sense of self!* Dreamless nights, I imagined myself on the clearer side of the glass. An expert adult, even-pulsed, all filled up and watching only her own.

Evenings my husband coached the competitive team. He trained girls to overcome the body's natural limits: pain, height, attention span, everything unmanageable and clumsy. Toddler moms whispered requests for him to gauge the future talent of their offspring: *What chance did they stand? Be honest.* He prodded teenage girls past "personal best." Often he went shirtless—through his own training regime and caloric math, he'd cultivated handsome swellings. Still, many nights he fretted over his flawless, fatless pecs and abs.

At home in flimsy bathroom light, he'd finger back and forth an indentation of his deltoid, memorizing it with his index, saying *Fuck genetics* and vowing to work harder.

I attempted to distract him with my body, but found naked, preposterous ways to fail against the shower wall, on our kitchen linoleum, across the reupholstered hulk of sofa, in the bucket seat of his chipped vintage car. One night I blocked his path to the bathroom, hands pressed against the doorway frame, my body a solid and impassible thing. He knelt before me, brought his breath nearer. His palms made slow appraisal of my hips, startled the backs my thighs, flushed their way to the front. When his fingers clinched the crease between leg and hip, he paused, counted pulses. "Heart rate's elevated enough to cut your BMI," he said. "I'll calculate how to curb your carb intake."

We splintered. I borrowed a friend's address. My husband parked his car against mine in the gymnasium lot and when my birthday arrived, not yet thirty, he arranged presents on the passenger seat for me to find. Joke gifts, I guess, unless you're six: Easy-Bake Oven, strawberry-scented pencils, a plastic cotton candy machine. Weeks later, the same seat: divorce papers I'd filed. Then he took the team away to compete at regionals. I worked extra hours, practiced the splits. I sucked helium for the kids and did handstands against blatant yellow walls until blood thrummed against my eardrums and the arms of the clock unspun. I ran dizzy till I shrank, until my uniform deflated.

A shiny, aweless girl from a competing gym arrived one night to try the place out. She said little, strode across the mats without asking, back arced in confidence. Her parents adored from the stands; I trailed. Gym emptied of all but us, I steeled myself beneath her while she casted on the bars, my arms out, hopeful like I waited for someone to arrive. She angled expert, gaining momentum as she executed each giant swing, pirouetted at the top of the bar, twisted into a double front flyaway. I wanted to catch her, but she defied catching. She defied mistakes and mistaking. And if she were to fall, I knew I'd fail us both.

The team triumphed home in a van, necks ringed with ribbons. Their parents received them in the lobby with banners and balloons and they put their hands on my husband, laying claim in their congratulations. I couldn't hear them behind the glass, but they now knew winning, all of them, and it was on to State where marble trophies waited, and I wondered about their miniscule hungers, where in the body that appetite swells and how big. My husband and I were that age when we'd met, but we were unaccomplished trivial kids. We attempted and exerted, but not utmost or damndest, and when our brief moments arrived spotlighted as they would before they wouldn't anymore, we failed to stick our landings—the only moment anyone remembers.

The expert girl's parents witnessed the celebration. They paid the insurance fee and signed a release form that night. When the families and my almost-over husband floated out into the lot, I chugged cherry codeine and ran the vacuum in the moonlight. I hung from the high bar. Gravity tugged my dense adult weight, and I endeavored to land in the dark.

PART THREE

PILLAR OF SALT

WHEN A NEW MAN TOUCHES ME, I become something else. Sometimes I become my sister, though I don't have a sister anymore.

There I'll be, parked in the driveway of a certain house in a dark car on a full moon, something of his bordering on something of mine—flesh between hip and belly, collarbone that refused to fuse post-accident—and if I'm my sister (and I usually am), I'll find the fleshy nub of his fingertip between my teeth, bitten. Sometimes it ends right there.

But unless it's his driveway, the certain driveway is my parents' driveway, and the gravel crunches below the tire as the car sways. A doctor prescribed parental supervision post-accident until the windshield and I sort ourselves out: I traveled through it, now it travels and travels through me. Some mornings I'll wake to find a shard of sunlight falling across my chest and, glinting next to me, a piece of glass that loosed itself like a tooth.

Sometimes I become an orange, peeled from the waist up, round against two palms.

Sometimes I'm a nesting doll, all hand-painted veneer, the real me five times inside.

Sometimes from the parking lot of the grocery store, I watch a bag boy corral silver carts like animals. When his shift's over, he might drive me someplace. These men are men of few syllables. "Be sweet." "Take care." We'll drive in silence. Then I'll say, "Pull over." He'll skid to a downhill slope of pines or patch of gravel at the edge of a cornfield. Then there on the ground I'll change from one thing to the next.

Like a pillar of salt.

Today the bag boy and I were unwedged, undressed, pinned by an empty sky. He said, "That blue's not convincing." Then he rolled onto his elbows, pointed up the road.

A family sat in the median grass, the trinity of mother, father, kid. They'd spread a blanket, basketless, near an assemblage of plastic flowers. I saw a white cross staked behind them. I put my shirt back on.

TEMPORARY RIVER

WE LAID DOWN SISTER. We became. The light stayed on. I painted the light that happens inside grocery stores. We learned to mask, we learned the Tunnel of Love. We saw inside other towns, some beds, events together threaded, the hospital sewing miniature light. I was ready. I swallowed red letters from Edison, my body seemed to flicker with my name. We memorized a sleep on rocks. The light stayed on.

I learned to sister. We played water tower. I took the light, it stayed, the mystery, the light letters from Edison with my name on them. We chased a river, we played blue pills, we seemed to flicker to the truth, we fused back water. The town got red letters. The light stayed on.

I took darkness into corners, stood up, slept less, existed between events. I rode the light life. The hospital sewed the light back on. I painted other lights, I painted the hospital, played games, existed in grocery stores. Existed between the pleasure. We had a town safe. We saved the Tunnel of Love; we went father, mother, brother, brother, sister, sister.

I moved faster, faster. Sister stayed painted in the light, stayed on the roof, in some beds, in prayer, in light sleep. I painted the failed light. We landed back together, my temporary. The mystery bones fused back now.

I learned in other towns, I packed boxes. Parents deflated, a father, a mother, I the light, I: miniature. I got tears, nothing happened.

But see the dark flicker? The light life and the dark don't go together. We darked and anything failed. The light was older, the other light events unbearable. Sister burned out. Faster, I packed up bones, games, pleasure. I swallowed red faster, I moved faster. Light was older. The Tunnel of Love flickered. The light played dark games.

We landed unbearable, but I swallowed red. We had chased. I had stayed on. I had stayed light. We stood up, we burned out, the light we knew lay down.

I packed our boxes, sister. We existed, sister.

MAN FOUND DEAD IN GRAVEYARD

THE IRIS, says the newsflash, is a thumbprint. When I rub fists to eyelids I follow a river down a blank tunnel. Reemerged, I'm unspecified in an unlit town, atop a hill, washing myself in a river of irises. (I fingered that flower once, an iris. Split the petal across my thumb like skin on skin and never touched one again).

From a friend, I received a sketch of a face: HAVE YOU SEEN THIS MAN? The man who shows up in dreams? The same man materializes behind thousands of lethargic eyes. Dreamers come forward saying they recall his gaze, he's their ex-this/that, he's maybe a man they used to know. They flash his photograph.

When I dream, it is usually this place, readymade: a hill I inhabit, with room for someone unexpected to wash up. Sometimes we build rivers together, hand over hand pushing water through an open tunnel. Or we pinch the petals off flowers, counting.

A small act, just dismantling blooms on a hill I know.

With my eyes closed, it's not my place to say who belongs where. Man on map. Man with hat in hand. "Man found dead in graveyard," said the newscast. His corpse splayed like a serious star. Amid flowers, I imagine, amongst moonlight, that perpetual bluish cemetery hue even in daytime.

They didn't say whether the man's eyes were closed or concealed with a hat. I picture some gesture of sleep: hat over face, mouth agape, maybe hand concealing eyes. Like a man who didn't collapse but lay down. Knowing which tunnel to follow, catching up to our resting eyes like a river.

NEIGHBOR RECALLS THE ACTORS

THEY WORE SOLDIERS' SUITS, never mind rain spoiling their fake brass medals green. Crop dusters floated above us advertising national sodas and elite hair care products. So much illogical beauty misted down like vapor trails. So much sadness mobilized above backyards like bad coughs. The neighbor told me he gets nervous after a few drinks. He wants someone to say to him, "Nothing yet is fucked." Words passed between us while, outside, banners in the sky receded for the evening. Then the sun dropped, as if handled by an efficient prop manager.

THE TIGER

THE TIGER DREAMED of air conditioning and, hungry also for a name, surrendered. Twice daily: tins of lifeless meat. Twice daily: a howling cloud of faces. He grew fond of municipal tranquilizers, the occasional red scarf tickling his cage, and television, where the very idea of tigerness had bloated and cartooned. One morning, the neighbor's son reached his hand toward the silver tin. From the tiger's foggy sleep, he heard the boy's heart. Later, the tiger would claim a breeze had urged him over the bars, not the memory of pursuit.

THE WOMEN

THE SKY WEAKENED with twilight, rain. Wasn't there a sopped and sloppy phrase: *Home is where you hang your head?* The rain became snow and the snow became women—he held his palm out, their nakedness heavier than he'd thought. They curved mid-air, hair upflaring. He tried to catch just one but each melted, leaving his hand damp and bruised. Meanwhile, she'd maintained disappointment beneath porch lights. She asked, "What did you bring me?" His arms had nothing to say for themselves. There was one box labeled "mine," another labeled "yours." In the driveway, his car's hatch looked like a mouth with no sound.

STAR CHILDREN

GREAT-GRANDFATHER WAS THE GRANDFATHER of neon. They say he invented it in a shed in a yard just like this one. He excelled at bending light into colors and shapes. He used glass globes and metal tubes to talk to stars in outer space. He taped the conversations, which he stored in a blue suitcase like this one. He called us Star Children. "Come here, Star Children," he'd call to us from the shed. When he was sober, he made divinity candies. They looked like miniature clouds.

UNTITLED WITH FATHER

HOW MANY BEES DIED in the honey? *This honey?* Yes, in this jar—how many bees died here? *I don't see any bees in the honey.* But some bees die in the honey, don't they? *No, I think they die afterward, maybe from exhaustion.* When they make the honey, do they know they're going to die? *No, they probably operate from instinct.* But they know they're making a sacrifice, don't they? *Yes, they spend their lives choosing one experience.* And refusing many others? *Yes, but of all things that were not wrong when you were young, did you have any favorites?* When you came through the door after you'd been away with work. *Because you thought I wouldn't come back?* No, because you were singing as though your life had never happened to you.

GAME SHOW

SOMEONE WITH TICKETS to a game show said, "Oh!" The man with tickets said, "Be honest." Said: "Midwestern beauty, one of many." My brand-new boots were white. When they wooed me stage-side, I lied. About my last name first. About my handshake last. About my legs and my laugh. I guessed the correct prices for batteries, surgeries, expressionless art collections. I guessed Otis Redding, I guessed Arlington, I guess I had something in my bag: a bottle, a cap, some rope, a brick, oh applause, the consequence of purple jacarandas radiating in the Studio 10 parking lot. The sign said CLAP HERE NOW. They complied. It was timed. The sign said THERE'S SO MUCH MORE I WANT TO SAY. I guessed Ajax, I guessed nine times nine. I guess your letter sank to the bottom of my bag like a rock. Like a chunk of porcelain, like a handful of song. Like the families eating dinner in silence and watery game show light. I guessed that night some men were nobodies in the nobody dark. Apologies for saying it like that, because they could breathe through masks and wander dust, and from that distance, the Earth might as well have been a shotgun wedding chapel. I guessed 1969. I guess my hand was a fist. I guessed "___." I guess I had something in my eye like stage light. I guessed it was summertime back home and picking strawberries and my bathing suit lost on the front lawn. I guessed jacaranda, a genus. I wanted to say, "My records melted like tar on a road." I wanted to say, "I can blink and make the studio audience drown." I wanted to guess right. Someone gave me tickets to a game show. The sign said CLAP HERE NOW. They complied. I guess I guessed wrong. It was timed.

NEIGHBOR CONSIDERS THE YARD AT MIDNIGHT

THE FROSTED LAWN is dotted with rabbits. The rabbits refuse to move. Learning is painful.

UFO

EVERYTHING that happens out-of-doors needs an explanation: on the other end of the field, I can already hear us ending happily. Let's say the field is a surface of water complicated by moonlight. The neighbors' dog dragged a long bone around the floor as you changed the station from static to static and back.

From the sky, the cornfield is an advertisement for emptiness or the even coat of a yellow dog. From the front yard: a puzzle solved by stillness. The rows become tunnels and blonde women wagging their fingers. When children go missing, it is through these dark mouths. This is what adults whisper when you're not in the room.

PINK WATER

THEN THE DISASTER HAPPENED. I was the opposite of innocent, selling products like a fraud, and I'd memorized the beauty specifics: pink cakes of cheek color with suggestive names, corrective pastes in heavy pots, authentic bovine eyelashes and tubes of organic glue. My high heels blistered the backs of my ankles. Nights, I was companionless in a drafty, cramped apartment next to the racetrack. Sleepless, I considered fate over the sounds of a streaming sitcom next door, wondered about the return counter when we die. "Heaven," claimed the model in soft-focus ads streaming nonstop each shift, "is beauty made more beautiful." She disappeared inside pink cotton candy clouds before it repeated.

When the most anticipated product launched, they made us say French phrases to customers who didn't speak French. The pink mist promised to make your face ethereal. Even skeptics pounced: lines formed beyond mall doors before we opened, before the music flooded down, before I powered the monitors filled with the pink cloud lady and her elevated cheekbones. Some customers seemed rich while others didn't. I spritzed their faces with pink water and pressed samples into their palms.

After a few days, my pale uniform had turned pinker and pinker. There was no escaping the stuff. I said, "Voilà" and went to sleep each night rehearsing vague prayers and hearing echoes of the cash register. I pictured myself as a single drop of pink water that would someday merge with other drops the same color. How beautiful, I thought, to become wholer than whole.

Some women bought bottles of product like they were drinking it. Like they existed in the desert and these colored drops could sustain them. My feet bled. My hands stained and burned. When a fresh truckload of product arrived, I waited with my co-worker on the loading dock. She preened in the sun and said, "Notice anything?" She was newish, her fake French worse than my own. I hadn't learned her name. But she was right—something had changed. "You look familiar," I said, and she threw her head back and laughed as if I were filming her.

One day, a woman stood at the counter. "I'm returning this," she said and pushed a bottle toward me. "Je suis désolée," I said. "That's against our policy." This was less than honest, but I didn't like her sourness, her mean mouth. I felt a damp spot in my left shoe and the pain of it compelled me to toughen. In the video ads, multiples of the same swinging woman tossed their heads back in slow-motion laughs, their feet bare, the earth miles below them as they ascended toward who knows where.

The woman raised both fists. I flinched and braced for the blow, but she pounded instead the glass case that separated us. She did it once—firm, hard, less than controlled—and it cracked beneath her hands. Veins traveled the glass and I tried to remember corporate protocol. We'd never discussed this. I could call security, I guessed, or throw my shoes in the trash and run home. But the woman smoothed her hair and left without another word.

"Bitch," my co-worker said as she sprayed the customer in her chair. "Bitch," the customer echoed beneath her. Neither of them looked up. They didn't know the glass case would shatter minutes later. My heart pumped quick blood that pulsed in my ears. Movements slowed, seconds cracking into less than seconds and I watched my coworker bend to the woman's face and pat it dry like she was blessing her. They were transfixed by one another, by "the process." There they were, and they were becoming one another, and they were becoming the others and they were beautiful in the same way, their faces permanently changed, their smiles never to leave them. "Tu es belle," my co-worker said, and the woman tilted back in the chair and tossed her hair and laughed.

When the counter shattered, they replaced it with another. It happened in slow motion: each of us becoming her. Oh, so becoming. Watch us floating up, up, up, our beautiful face trapped inside this beautiful frame.

ASSEMBLED

After Charles Simic

IT WAS TENTATIVE, how I assembled myself. The way a box fan picks up radio stations to piece together shreds of evening news in the dusk of an emptied living room.

I heard my neighbors rustle against each other like wet leaves. It was the part of the test I tend to fail. I slept alone, on the verge of someone's shadow. I walked Speed Avenue as families ate silent dinners in simple light.

A man smoking beneath the movie theater's sign said that the pearl is the oyster's autobiography. But I could have it backwards. Couples filed from the dark, squinting into daylight. They looked beautiful, harmless as dazed babies.

I had interviewed for a job selling expensive rugs.

The air conditioners of our city thrust the grid into sudden blackout. I drank behind the grocery with my brother, who worked there for beer money. One night I passed a guy sprawled shirtless on his lawn. He lifted his head to say, "We are the last of the free Americans."

Because I believe all objects are infused with the divine, I took a job at a department store cosmetics counter. Some women knew what they wanted, but most looked shamed beneath the lamps, asking me which shades would make them prettier.

At night I shed the uniform, a squared-off lab coat. I scrubbed away lipstick and mascara over one of the double sinks. The water was the color of a dark, wet road. The raw face approximating one I recognized.

PUTTING THE NEIGHBORS TO BED

THE PERFORATIONS that had always been began to show: the limp sponge of father's heart as he strode toward the phone, the bottom line of mother's getaway fund. Whispers traveled the vents from sister's basement floor: a neighbor boy scrabbling against the window, the cringe of the liquor cabinet door.

The moon looked flat. Brisk wind swiped buds from stems.

Next door, a neighbor sang through the open window of his shower. The music suggested opera, Italian. He didn't tell his wife he knew the notes in words that she would understand. "Sing it that way," she'd say. "Sing it again." He was afraid the beauty might be lost in her.

RENDEZVOUS

THERE I GO AGAIN, falling out of your unforgettable breath. The finest doors opened at an unprecedented pace, but joy and happiness have been, not are. I ask if you want reality candlelit, if you want me tethered by the coattails all well, unspoiled, if you want a location so I won't run away. I will stay clear and in hand, even though it's a little picture postcard. Even though it's your personalized reluctance. Even though it's I'm trying to catch you. Just ask if you want miles of an unbelievably bitter sea then that is what you'll get. Remind me what made you so special. That hotel, those couples hurting in rooms of luxury.

PERFECT CHRISTMAS

OUR TOWN had a church called Perfect Christmas. It was Baptist or Protestant, I forget which. There were glitter crosses nailed to the walls, Christmas lights across the rafters, and sprigs of holly no matter how hot it got. Beneath the roof's nasty leak: the manger with a baby Jesus. He smiled through his damp face. He smiled in his perfect sleep because he hadn't suffered yet.

I quit Perfect Christmas during Missing Summer. We called it that because it was almost fall and also because people kept disappearing. There was the neighbor and his homemade plastic plane. There was the boy who huffed that nasty paint.

There were others, too, but they've disappeared even further.

I bought a Ouija Board with money I got for watching my brother. I'd latch my bedroom door during storms and steer the plastic heart-shaped oracle. I'd ask it to spell out radio lyrics or nasty words or assurances. I kept my fingertips light, tried not to push it. The closest to a perfect word: H-E-L. "Hello," I imagined someone said above.

The TV was nasty that fall, filled with shitty news and glittery costumes and storm warnings. One day my sleeping brother drifted from its glow. He walked out into the wet road. He walked the white line like a smiling drunk. I tried to pull him home, but his slick skin slipped through my fingertips.

This happened all Missing Summer long and then it was winter. I returned to Perfect Christmas one last time. I'd shoved the board away, a stupid toy, and wore my best dress, a little vulgar now in its shortness. I pressed my palms together and suffered beneath the glittering lights. They were cheap, I could see that now. On the verge of burning out. Everything on the verge of burning out, except for the sleeping plastic baby with the rain on his face, something I might save.

DIARY OF AN EX-PRECEDENT

THE SUN COLLAPSED mid-river. News soothed our stricken bridge commute: tributes to Ronald Reagan, Monday mergers that sent stocks diving, strikes and dissent. Melancholy pictures from space with their attendant ultimatums and warnings.

They drove past me: men and women checking their heartbeats and pulses, a generation of optimists waiting to be wrong. We wore our silver linings on our sleeves. We figured we broke it, we'd buy it.

It is supposed to be the last day on Earth, according to math and our physician-medium's chartings. But today in the Ganges they found a fish that can repair the human heart. We are the generation that failed swim class because we couldn't hold our breath—and here we are, floating. It is not the end of the world.

PART FOUR

THE HOLE

MY FATHER RESTS HIS CHIN on the shovel's handle. The hole before him begs to be deeper. Gone already: redbud trees, patches of violet peeled away like a bandage. Goodbye, ragged hammock. Goodbye, tire swing. My father used to be President of the Neighborhood Homeowner's Association. He doesn't know he's been impeached. Neither "neighbor" nor "impeached" mean anything. My mother mostly looks out the window. She's become Special Occasion religious. She parts the red kitchen curtains and says "Jesus Christ" in a voice reserved for car accidents. She wakes me in the night to help her apply Special Occasion makeup. My brother counts the shovel strikes aloud. Shovel dings rock: a star collapsing. My father tells us kids not to go anywhere, we have to take turns guarding the hole. When a bagger at the grocery asks me to the movies, I tell him I'm busy. "I hope it's not too dangerous," he says. My brother, sister, and I rig a rappelling device. At the bottom of the hole we shine like dimes. My brother was born with gills, remnants like pinpricks above his ears. My sister can float like a kite—the year she turned thirteen, we kept a rope around her waist. When the hole reaches beyond the sides of the house, my mother no longer believes it will bring us the forgiveness each of us needs. She packs a suitcase, calls a cab, waits at the end of the driveway. I part the curtains with my hands. I hold my breath until she has gone. I fall asleep. I dream of boats. The hole has become a lake. The hole has become a breathing body. The current drags lawn chairs across our neighbor's yard. My father is gone. I step off the porch into chin-deep water. I duck below the surface, grab my brother's waist, kick. In the sky above, our pajama-footed sister waves us east.

FATHER'S ELEGY FOR SATISFACTION

THE PILLS THAT POPULATE the cabinet start with the end of the alphabet. Solved for X or Z: they enumerate our separate sleeps. The radio instructs us to stay inside: lawns have been canceled, and now crop dusters dive low to eradicate new symptoms from our neighborhood. Red dust covers our roofs like rust, but gentle. Tire swings drop from the weight and roll. The next-door neighbor threatens tree limbs with a Father's Day saw. The tune: primitive as teeth on wood. Beneath his rubber mask, he's neither laughing nor exhaling.

Holding our breath: popular as family pastimes go when just last year we shared the same last name. Now the kids have each chosen their own. I grow nostalgic for the years I can't remember. Sure, the carpet had bruise-shaped stains from wine, the children's sentences rough and unintelligible. Sure, annuities grew softer, vacations to the shore a little shorter. But those sunsets from our separate hotel rooms? The lullaby of offshore drilling as we dreamed of one another?

Sometimes I doze as I drive uphill to work each morning. The street a haze of semi-solid shapes that feel familiar: the sudden blooms of shrubs, those boxes filled with disappearing letters. Curb, streetlamp, phone booth, neighbor. There's a word for this kind of sleep you shoulder like a granite stone until it falls and disappears a year behind you. Like family albums filled with snow, or that old joke when less than no one's in the picture. In my hands the covers become fictionless, less plastic. They turn to leather from a once-astonished animal.

STILL LIFE WITH NEIGHBOR

THE NEIGHBOR OCCURRED from the south. The neighbor occurred from Hollywood. The neighbor managed a cattle ranch. The neighbor produced game shows. The neighbor is credited with the phrase "lemons to lemonade." The neighbor has never thrown the baby out with the bathwater. The neighbor shingled the roof himself. The neighbor carved the fountain himself. The neighbor used to have a wife. The neighbor's wife: disappeared/deceased. The neighbor's wife jumped from the roof. The neighbor's wife simply fell. She lived three weeks, in a hospital, not in this town. The officers declared it an accident. The officers declared it a non-accident. The neighbor has no children because his wife is ex- or dead. The neighbor lets kids cut through his yard. The neighbor places candy in their hands on Halloween. The neighbor once chased a child from his porch. The neighbor doesn't act right around children. The neighbor doesn't act right around adults. The neighbor doesn't add up. The neighbor can be observed from the house next door. The yard next door is empty: there has never been a house. There has never been a neighbor, but you think of him just the same.

AT THE BEACH

WE ARE PUTTING SOMETHING to each other and I am waiting for you to say something round. Breasts, maybe asses. I say fingers, but I'm thinking necks. We play this game as we watch expensively constructed women neglect their babies. The babies splash around in tide pools that have been declared off-limits by the State Ecological Society. The tide pools are jackpots brimming with starfish spines and the lapping tongues of anemones—so many unformed bodies—and now they are brimming with babies, another type of body. The women don't get too near the babies or the water because it will disappear something delicate that has refused to leave them.

You say, "I touched a woman like that once." You say: "We're surrounded by wrists so fragile and worth so much." I fall into my towel, dream of high school. From the concession stand where I sold sno cones on Saturday nights, I had memorized the identically tanned necks of two umpires. They were brothers who came to my window at night, knocked on the glass. "Their names began with a C," I tell you. But this might not be true because, although I'm saying C, I am thinking necks, nothing more nothing less.

When the sun arrives directly overhead you tell me that the women's beauty will refuse to leave us. Babies, round and happy, buoy insignificantly. Sleeping lifeguards dream of indoor employment. You twist a finger into mine. Then through the back of my head, hooking into the soft spot.

SO MANY BONES

THE LAST TIME I SAW my father it was over the fence that separated our yards. "I'm sorry I never told you my real name," he said. "That's okay," I replied. Dogwoods frothed above us. He said, "I'm sorry I never told you I had joy in my life, like seeing it written on a piece of rice when I was a kid." He turned away from me, and I wanted to say something, but it was getting very dark and very cold and I still had so many bones to rake up.

IN THE SHAPE OF A-OK

I COUNT IT AS LUCKY, the mate-less glove punctuating the sidewalk, that severed hello of a stranger left for me to find. And the egrets above, only marginally migratory, unbunching against the aluminum sky in the shape of a checkmark, in the shape of an A-OK, in the shape of mating for life, in a sigh of relief. Never mind that they rhyme with "regret."

Over dinner a friend offered me his microscope, through the lens of which one can observe the skittish, desultory tendencies of cells. But I'd seen them before, had to memorize their names in high school. There: the one that craves a hand at the small of the back. There: the one that dreams of crushing bird eggs in my palms. There: the one responsible for the perception of checkmarks.

At the restaurant, a friend offered me her head. As we stood side-by-side the superior specimen became obvious. She dreams in clover. She doesn't crush things. Even in monotone bar light, her eyes flash like heads-up pennies I'm urged to snatch.

Etched in myelin, undeniable: bird-crusher, thief. So I walk home from the restaurant backward, the proactive version of looking over my shoulder. I sling salt from a stolen shaker. And from every car that passes, someone waves, I swear it. From the window of every car that passes: someone with her fingers crossed.

SLEEP

THERE IS NOTHING like falling asleep in your childhood home, nestled among wet hills. With blankets pulled to your lips you dream of knots in the apple tree, broken bones, the schoolyard sky dressed in cemetery blue. The familiar blanket is heavy and you're restless even as you rest. The sheep count you.

BULLSHIT FENCES

I TRAVELED toward the Tunnel of Love. I gripped a wire fence down a gritty road. Rough cars flurred by on bald tires and my hand buzzed like it was drunk. All around me the Sunday feeling, a pale yellow of temporary comfort.

I wanted to whisper something breakable into the Tunnel of Love.

I wanted to whisper my *sister* or *whiskey* or directions.

I was dying for Sunday Tunnel of Love forgiveness.

I'd heard that the Tunnel of Love could hear me.

K. appeared from behind a stand of black trees. I followed her through the rust fence and into a thicket. She said, "So many bullshit fences in this town. I got tangled and forgot where I was going."

I understood bullshit fences. Our town was choked

with them. In some places (the bank, the church) they crossed and tangled.

"I'm traveling toward the Tunnel of Love," I told her. "Know the way?"

"The ride with dark water?"

"Yes," I said. "It's Sunday and I plan to be forgiven."

An ambulance plowed through the woods. It crushed black branches as it traveled. When it stopped, a man rolled down the window. Far from casual, he was a doctor. Far from a stranger, he was a doctor my scars remembered.

"I'm lost," he confessed, hopeless. "There's been an accident. I cut through a fence, but I can't find my way through these black trees."

In that moment I understood that I would not travel to the Tunnel of Love, that the Tunnel of Love was more than a day's walk away, that I'd been wrong. "I can show you out," I said.

I climbed into the passenger's seat. "Drive toward those sparks," I said. Fireworks erupted like dendrites in the direction of the county reservoir, reds and blues even in daylight.

He flipped a switch and sirens screamed. The sun shimmered across the windshield like the surface of water. He jacked the pedal hard. Bullshit fences smeared into one another: stone, steel, brick, electric, gold, even glass, which could break, again and again, but resurrect. I closed my eyes and imagined a ride. Oh, I was on a slow sightless journey, floating through tunnel darkness, water lapping. Guilt damp on my skin like evidence. Alone with my grief. Alone to be released. Alone so nobody had to witness the bullshit confines of the bullshit choices I'd once made.

IMAGINARY WHEAT

IN THE ABSENCE OF SLEEP I conjure pastoral landscapes glazed with the warmth of 1980s television. My brother calls. He's not sleeping either. A candy-colored nuclear sunset has obliterated his identical field of imaginary wheat.

When we were children, we were afraid of the neighbors. My brother told me stories until the house locked itself to sleep. Now he's afraid of the end of the world. He tells me how to boil water in the woods. It's hard to sleep with the news of our impermanence. It is love that makes our voices shiver.

I want to ask my neighbor if he worries about the end of the world. When I put my hand to the wall, I am comforted by the black-and-white static of his sleep. I want to tell him I'm not afraid of him. I want to ask: "Are the church bells songs of a sleeping house, furniture gliding back and forth across an empty hall?"

All these years, I've been afraid of sunset. I want to confess to my neighbor that I don't believe my brother. I want to confess that I'm becoming permanent. I'll say: "The more permanent I become, the less sleep I get."

The conversation will make us both uncomfortable, but my neighbor believes in happy endings. I can hear it in his face. In the morning, he'll see my open palms and wonder what I want to borrow. We'll wade a prayer into early morning television wheat. All the locks of the neighborhood obliterated, shivering.

FORTY-LOVE

THE MEN HAD GONE. Now it was default ladies' night. I danced despite myself in that remaindered room. We rollicked and sweated. I caught my breath at the edge of the bar as music traveled my damp neck, chest. I sucked ice chips each time my drink dried.

"You like strawberries?" a woman asked. She slid between my knees. She tickled my nose with pink dust then flicked the feather up my thigh. I closed my eyes. I pictured snow melting the moment it touched warm concrete. "Stick out your tongue," she said.

The pill she halved tasted like baby stuff, medicine disguised as candy, and the piece hung inside my throat before dissolving. I followed her into the bathroom. She smacked the heater on the wall before she locked us into the only empty stall.

Then the dance floor was filled with glistening strawberry dolls, an extinct scent I remembered from playgrounds, but we were the opposite of pulseless and we were covered in glittery dust. I supposed every one of us was gorgeous. The men—wherever they floated now—missed us, I was sure of it. I considered my mother, how her young self would have loved this, would have dabbed my eyeshadow beneath the light's flash, would have whispered something rotten, something funny.

I needed to tell her. I needed to reveal that I was made of little more than water. I wanted to impart my heart's survival and I was an animal that couldn't wait until morning. I counted my month's money and flagged a cab in the dark.

The city turned into town and the town turned into country as the driver sped past dead patches of corn. "This'll cost you," she said through the scratched plastic pane and she tapped the meter to prove it. What I said, I don't remember.

I arrived at my mom's bed. She was a memory so familiar that she became abstract if I considered her for more than a moment. "You," she said, opening her eyes. I worried that she could see how fast my veins slung blood, how my body surged with purpose. I'd forgotten why I came.

She drove us to the tennis courts, she in pajamas beneath her coat, me covered in strawberry sparkles, barely covered at all in my party skirt. The swings looked miniature in the dark dawn, but so did the trees, so did the road. A crow hovered above the court, the only bird alive, and shouldn't that species be extinct by now? My mother called across the net. Her voice traveled through the body of the bird.

She served. Each ball was a memory my body tensed to smash as the snow came at a sharp angle and stung my bare legs. It was really falling now, heavier and thicker all around us, and it would stay. I ran to my mother.

"My heart," I said.

"I know," she said. "Forty-love."

THE NEW YEAR

BEYOND CHRISTMAS TREE LOTS, at the edge of what little light we had left in our country, we found the New Year frozen to the beach. Beyond it what was nothing looked completely still. A train whistled a distant anthem. It got dark, as they say. Midnight, we discovered one friend, then another, rumoring between black pines, pressed together beneath moon regret, strolling against snow. In the back of my sleep: an engine. No territories crossed, but something warm inside me moving.

HORSESHOES

WHAT WE NAIL TO CREATURES to keep them steady rarely works: hold still, we say with blunt and heavy hammers.

Good luck.

ACKNOWLEDGMENTS

My enormous thanks to Benjamin DeVos at Apocalypse Party Press for his generosity and care for this book. I also owe much gratitude to Roxane Gay, Allison Wright, Michael Seidlinger, and The Accomplices for their support of this work. Thank you to my teachers and fellow writers at SU, and special thanks to Christopher Kennedy for his wisdom and guidance. To Ryan, my family, and friends: thank you.

Acknowledgments are made to the following publications in which these pieces first appeared, sometimes in slightly different forms or under slightly different titles:

The Broken Plate, The Collagist, Corium, DIAGRAM, DOGZPLOT, elimae, Everyday Genius, Eye for an Iris, Faultline Journal of Arts and Letters, Fractured West, Gigantic, HOBART, Housefire, I'M SORRY, I THOUGHT THIS WAS AMERICA, Juked, Kitty Snacks, Many Mountains Moving, Metazen, Nano Fiction, NAP, The One Three Eight, PANK, Pindeldyboz, The Progressive, Six Sentences, Sixth Finch, SmokeLong Quarterly, Verbal Seduction, Wigleaf.

ABOUT THE AUTHOR

Ashley Farmer is the author of four books of poetry, fiction, and nonfiction. Her work has been published in places like *Gay Magazine, TriQuarterly, The Progressive, Buzzfeed, Flaunt, Nerve, Potomac Review, Gigantic, Salt Hill Journal, DIAGRAM,* and elsewhere. She is the recipient of Sarabande Books' 2020 Series in Kentucky Literature, *Ninth Letter*'s 2018 Literary Award in Creative Nonfiction, the *Los Angeles Review*'s 2017 Short Fiction Award, and fellowships from Syracuse University and the Baltic Writing Residency. Ashley lives in Salt Lake City, UT with the writer Ryan Ridge.

Printed in the USA
CPSIA information can be obtained
at www.ICGtesting.com
LVHW021337301124
797960LV00003B/483